LIVING WITH
THE DEAD

LIVING WITH THE DEAD

(The Tale of Old Corpsenberg)

DARRELL SCHWEITZER

Introduction by Tim Lebbon

Cover and Illustrations by Jason van Hollander

WILDSIDE PRESS

Published by Wildside Press LLC.
wildsidepress.com | bcmystery.com

INTRODUCTION

I should warn you, the story you're about to read is a strange one indeed, and if you have any preconceptions—either after seeing the title or cover, or reading the first couple of pages—throw them out of the window right now.

Because you'll be refreshingly, pleasingly wrong.

Actually, a lot of what this book is about is defying expectations, and having the knowledge and courage necessary to carve your own destiny. Clever, eh? Indeed, as I was reading this novella for the first time, 'clever' is the one word that kept leaping to mind. And thoughts like that always make for a nice reading experience especially when, as in this case, I'm reading a writer for the first time. I've met Darrell a few times, and I'm aware of his award-winning work as an essayist, critic and editor of *Weird Tales* magazine. But until now, he's always been on that very long 'must read soon' list in my mind.

When I read the opening paragraph, until the last line I was thinking *Oh hell, it's another zombie novella.* Not that I've anything against zombie stories, having written a couple myself, but as I started reading—knowing a little about Darrell, and having chatted with him a few times—I was expecting something a little more...out of the ordinary.

I'm glad to say, I certainly got that.

Clever chap, that Schweitzer.

* * * *

iving With the Dead is a strange, bizarre, surreal journey through the grim town of old Corpsenberg, a place where the order of things must be preserved...and where wonder and freedom are to be found in not doing so. The author's cleverness comes through in several ways, and I'll talk about them a little here...although I don't want to talk too much about the delights that await you, as this is one story that is definitely best discovered on your own.

Firstly, Darrell writes from several points of view, often retelling the same piece of action or interaction through different eyes. This is a neat way of getting deep into a character's head and revealing some of their hidden depths, and then immediately displaying how they are perceived and accepted—or not—by those around them. It's been done before, of course, but rarely to such great effect. And though this is a risky, audacious style, there's never the feeling that we're just rehashing old ground. The characters are dissimilar enough from each other that their understanding of events is diverse and revelatory. We see a school teacher, for example, and her desperate attempts to preserve the order of things; and then we see one of her pupils, and realise how the order of things is a prison.

Darrell is also very adept at world-building. This isn't just a case of describing a few buildings, a landscape, or how the two interact. There's a definite skill about creating a place as memorable as old Corpsenberg, a talent that requires richness and uniqueness of vision, combined with dexterity of language, to build a place that haunts you months or years after you've read about it. Anyone who has ever read Jeff Vandermeer's Ambergris stories, visited China Miéville's new Crobuzon, or has spent time in Gary braunbeck's Cedar Hill, will recognise such a sense about old Corpsenberg.

And the author is also skilled at planting ideas and offering tantalising glimpses beyond the world he is prepared to tell us about, and into whatever mysteries lie beyond. That's important, because any story benefits from a sense of a wider world existing around the action and events it describes. But in this tale especially—where the world is so strange, so ordered and so *contained*—the sense of something beyond is vital, and can be terrifying. It's also intriguing, frustrating and brilliantly realised. Again, I don't want to give away too much…but the ships that steam in and deposit their dead are, for me, the stuff of nightmares. Then there are the clouds, the tower, and…

But I don't want to say too much. This is a mysterious world you're about to enter, and you're going to be an outsider looking in. The more I tell you, the more you might feel like an insider from the first page.

And old Corpsenberg is not a place where any right-minded person would want to feel at home.

So what does it all mean? That's another of Darrell's enviable talents: challenging the reader. This novella is so filled with symbolism that, though always keen to read on, I found myself taking frequent pauses to absorb what I'd just read and try to fathom its meaning. This is not a simple, linear tale of cause-and-effect and beginning-middle-end, but a richly imagined dream-world of fantastic ideas, dark meanings, and moral challenges that both the characters and the reader must undergo. On a wider level, there's the comfort of routine and inherited beliefs which combine to stifle creative thinking and interrogative discussion. And on a narrower, more personal level, there are the trials faced by those characters who are…well…overwhelmingly *human* in their approach to the problems, inconsistencies and quirks they see in this, their strange world. They're told to act and think one way, to *preserve to order of things*, but you know that old saying: There's always one.

Despite the relative shortness of a novella, the world here is very intricately portrayed, the characters are vivid, and the reader is left with an appalling sense of painful history and futile futures. And yet running through the heart of *Living With The Dead* is the sense that something, perhaps everything, is about to change.

So welcome to the wonderful, unforgettable, dreadful town of old Corpsenberg.

The ships are sailing in.

And soon, it will be time to gather the dead.

Tim Lebbon
Goytre
January 2008

THE MOST BEAUTIFUL DEAD WOMAN IN THE WORLD

I

The dead come from the sea, at night. Of course no one ever witnesses their arrival, since it is the immemorial custom of our town, particularly on those nights of all nights, that everyone is snug in their bed, behind bolted doors and locked shutters. We know, not by any calendrical calculation, but merely by a feeling in the air, by an unbidden pause in rhythm of life itself, that such an advent is upon us. Then we wait, in silence, in the darkness, and, in silence and darkness, the dead arrive. We find them in the morning, on the docks, piled in great heaps like a catch of fish.

That is when I am called upon in my official capacity. On such mornings, it is my duty to arrive at the water's edge first, just at dawn, when I can still observe the black silhouettes of the ships which have delivered the dead to us, anchored off-shore, visible in the thinning fog.

This particular morning, I discern two tramp freighters. In ancient, mildewed paintings in the town hall, you can behold a similar scene, rendered in shades of grey, showing tall-masted ships with half-furled sails like stagnant clouds. I have no memory of ships like that, and I never asked my father about them, nor, I suspect, did he ever ask his. Thus are we left free of any disturbing hint of change; for, indeed, nothing changes in our town, save that the number of the dead who reside among us slowly increases beyond counting.

In the dim, cold morning, I stand on the dock in my black coat with its pewter buttons, in my dampstained bicorn hat which I inherited from my father (and he from his). As an official of the unseen government, I must preside, as the townspeople slowly emerge from their houses and process down to the docks, the looks on their faces as blank as those of the corpses. In fancy, once, I thought, *they are like condemned prisoners on the way to execution,* but, no, it was never like that, nor are they like hopeless slaves in a salt-mine. (I must have gotten these images from reading.) The better analogy is to the carven figures that move before the face of the great clock before the Town Hall: the reaper, the sower, the man with the shovel, the coachman driving his hearse. All these, unthinking, without volition, go about their business, complete their rounds, and so the cycle continues.

It is hardly necessary for me to do anything, that morning or any other. More for the comfort than anything else, for the sense that I am, as a representative of the unseen government, ca*pable* of giving direction, I walk among the crowds and heaps of corpses, pointing with my cane (which was my father's, and my father's father's) as if to say, without words, *You, take that one.*

One by one, the corpses are hauled away by the townspeople, who will carry them into their homes, set them up in positions of familiarity or comfort, accepting the dead as our guests and neighbors. Strong men sometimes heft one or two on their shoulders. You can see family groups with wheelbarrows or small wagons, piling on a load. This morning an old beggar woman, ragged, barefoot, soon to be a corpse herself, I suspect, grabs a dead child by the wrists and drags it off. She weeps softly, from unimaginable dreams or longings or simply from senility; I cannot know. But even this is part of the larger, inscrutable pattern of our existence, and I do not interfere.

And so it is, mere routine, until, as the corpses are uncovered, layer upon layer—*earthquake! cataclysm! She* is revealed: the body of a young woman (such as I am able to estimate age), whose face and features are, despite her sodden condition, *exquisite,* like some perfect marble statue, almost translucent from a sunrise gleaming behind it. (Not something I have ever seen, or even dreamed; again, perhaps, imagery from some crumbling book perused in the town library during my offduty hours.)

This is the beginning of my transgression, the mere sight of her, the *fascination.*

Hoping no one will notice, I pull her out of the heap, then stand with my feet on either side of her, as if I hope to hide her under my long coat, pretending she isn't there. With increased determination, I flick my cane this way and that, imposing the power of the unseen government to maintain the smooth flow of things. The process is concluded; the clockwork figures complete their rounds; and I stand alone, astride my beauty, on the deserted dock.

Now the sun has risen, as bright as it ever gets in our town. The fog is not quite dispelled, the sky still grey, but there is an increased light, and the black silhouettes of the freighters across the water have vanished.

Alone, then, I take up my prize in my arms, as if she were a living child. She weighs almost nothing. I am amazed by that, as I am at the beauty of her face and the perfection of her hands and feet (which are bare and muddy; she wears only a tattered white gown). I am frightened at the way my heart races so, out of fear, out of dread of detection, yes, but moreso out of the terror of the discovery *of myself*, as if, from a dream, with this beautiful one in my arms, I have awakened into some wholly new and different reality.

The touch of her is neither warm nor cold. I feel almost no sensation as I carry her, save her wet hair touching my cheek, shifting slightly as I walk.

Alone, then, for the townspeople have gone back to their homes to find places for the new arrivals, I make my way up the main street of our town, past the confectioner's shop, where the undecaying dead are set in the bay window, around a little table, as if enjoying cakes and candies; past the shoe-maker's, where an old, white-bearded man sits in a chair above the door, held in place by ropes, his feet dangling down to display the finest quality boots.

Others of the dead line benches, or sit in doorways. Some lie in heaps in the alleys, supposedly sleeping, but, disgraceful though it may seem, more like discarded trash. I know I should do something about that, deliver official complaints to certain persons, but I never have, and doubt I ever shall.

If there have ever been more zealous officials in our town, I do not know of them, nor did my father speak of any to me, or his father to him. With my beautiful dead one in my arms, I arrive, then, unchallenged, at my own dwelling, which is in a loft, reached by a winding exterior staircase, in the back of the Town Hall adjoining the clock tower. I ascend, drawing very near to the wooden figures of the town clock, which are nearly life-sized, but old and worn, their paint chipping off. (They rest in coffin-like niches when the mechanism has not called them up before the clock face to perform their circumambulations.) A pigeon roosts on the hearse-driver's upraised whip-hand.

I heft my beloved onto my shoulder until I can get my keys out, then fumble my way within. I set her down on the bed, then open the shutters to let the dim daylight in. A dozen dead faces stare at me from out of the shadows, my own company of guests, often those left behind on the docks when everyone else is gone. I have accumulated several old men and women, and a rather startling trio of little children, two boys and a girl, all with their throats cut. The dead crowd my shelves, occupy all my chairs, sit slumped in my corners.

I prop the new arrival up with pillows (all the while wondering where I am going to sleep from now on). I wrap her in my best sitting-robe, bathe and dry her poor feet and put socks on them, this deference intended to say to the others who share our quarters, *Look, this one is special. She is to be your queen.*

Which course is the continuation of my transgression, an actual crime now, for the ideology of our unseen government demands perfect equality among the living and the dead. We may have no queens here, any more than we may have a town official who claims one particular corpse for himself, guards it as jealously as a dog guards a bone, and so subverts the entire process whereby the dead come to rest in the *correct* place for each one of them.

Where this girl actually belongs, now, we shall probably never know.

But the mania is upon me and will not be denied. She is *mine*. My heart goes out to her, as if I could somehow return her to life, and she could indeed be my queen. I saw some discarded holiday decorations in the mud at the foot of the stairs. I run back down, snatch up some bright metal and streaming tinsel, then fashion them into a crown, which I place, with all reverence, upon my queen's head. I speak to her in tones

I never use toward any of my other guests—to whom I am polite, as duty requires, but nothing more—and, leaning forward to whisper in her perfectly-formed ear, pretending that I do so to prevent the other dead from eavesdropping, *I tell her that I love her.*

Have I completely lost my mind, all sense of propriety, any shred or remnant of social conscience?

Most likely it is so.

Even I am overwhelmed by the enormity of what I have done, and so I button up my great black coat again, place my hat on my head, and, with cane in hand, make my way down the stairs and into the street once more, where I spend the rest of the day going about my rounds, chatting amiably with the townspeople, observing how people go about their various duties. Mr. K—— sweeps his doorstep at a precise hour and minute, as he always does, whether there is anything to be swept from it or not. J——, the taximan, bawls out an absurd song as he wheels corpses about in his pedicab, sometimes pausing to point out this or that architectural feature or significant spot, as if he is a tour-guide.

The dead fill the shops, the restaurants, the library, the waiting room in the train station where the train never comes and only the dead have the patience to wait for it. (Once there was laughter in our town and this was seen as a joke. But I have heard no laughter, nor has my father described any to me, nor did his father speak of any to him.)

Mrs. Z—— complains that the children in the tiny school have to squirm sideways through masses of poorly placed, shabbily maintained dead to make their way into the schoolroom, where the students and teacher have to stand because all the desks are filled by corpses. I promise to investigate, and take my leave of Mrs. Z——. But, when the teacher sees me looking in through the window, she simply waves, and the children, listlessly, raise their hands.

All is as it has always been, as our unseen government requires, and so, without incident, I complete my rounds.

The town clock chimes the hour before curfew.

Somehow the day has passed. I don't remember most of it. I must have stopped for lunch somewhere along the way, probably at the usual tavern, operated by the redoubtable V——, where a corpse hangs in the place of a swinging sign, with bells tied around his ankles, jingling forlornly in the occasional breeze.

The day has passed unnoticed, I say, because my mind has been filled with passionate contemplation of what I have done, with *expectation* which rises to a point of frenzy. I am terrified for myself and of myself. I start in fright when I glimpse my own visage in a storefront mirror. If such a person could be walking through the streets of our town, garbed in the uniform of the highest authority…then I cannot even complete the thought, save to grope blindly toward the concept that existence is a meaningless horror which *provides no security* for either the living or the dead, if such undetected moral corruption is possible.

Yet at the same time I tell myself that my love for my queen is something new and wonderful, something beautiful, like an infusion of impossible *color* into our fog-bound existence, which is absurd, as if I were still young and capable of romantic feelings!

And yet I *am!* To compound my offenses, I snatch the entire wares of a dead flower-seller out of her dead hands, leaving no payment behind in her cup, and, furtively, I scuttle back up my stairs, past the disapproving, peeling faces of the clock-tower figures. Once more I fumble with my keys. My hands are cold. The damp evening air oppresses me. My teeth chatter.

Secretly then, ever so *secretly* I make my way inside, confident in the discretion of my other house-guests, and I strew the flowers across the bed in wild abandon, and then I fall to my knees and *worship* before this altar of absolute beauty! I spill out to my beloved all my longings, the story of my whole life, gushing about how when I was young I once dreamed of a place of green grass and sunlight, away from the dead. In grotesque profanation of the trust placed in me by the un- seen government, I have allowed such thoughts, dreams, or pseudo-memories to grow within me like a luminous cancer, rather than trying to purge myself through my work, as any responsible and moral person would at least try to do.

Dare I describe what follows? *I kiss her hand,* weeping, and eventually fall asleep on my knees, holding her hand in mine.

II

The Complete Confession of the Disgraced official, whose name has been expunged from all Town re- cords:

The miracle, I swear, was not a dream. It was far, far more than a dream.

I awoke in the timeless darkness of the night, and *felt her soft hands caressing the sides of my head.*

I beheld her face, as marble-pale as she had always been, but now positively *luminous,* as if the full, unshrouded Moon shone from within her. She returned my gaze. Our eyes met, locked, and our souls mingled together forever. She smiled gently.

Then she whispered my name, my full name, not just the letter of designation by which I am addressed in our town. Only a mother could know that, or a lover. I suppose I had whispered it to her, amidst my prior, frenzied discourse, which only confirmed my suspicion that she was, miraculously, *nei- ther dead nor alive,* but in a different, transcendent state. She could hear me as the dead cannot. She remembered, as the dead do not. She spoke in a voice like sweetest music.

Yet the touch of her hand was not cold, like that of a corpse, nor warm, like that of a living person.

It was almost as if she were not there at all.

But *no!* I will never accept that! not a dream. Not an hallucination. She was a *sending* from some power infinitely greater than even our hidden government, from some place beyond the fog from which the ships come, which no one in our town has ever imagined.

I bade her get up, and she got up, and we walked out of the room together. She took my hand in hers and we whirled, we *danced* to unheard music on the little landing at the top of the stairs, where the wooden clock-tower figures glared at us disapprovingly.

With flowers in her hair, the crown on her head, and her white gown trailing behind her, she raced through the streets, and called after me to follow, laughing. And laughing, I followed. At the establishment of the redoubtable V——, I unlocked the door, for as a minister of the unseen government I possessed the universal key to all locks in our town. Inside, we broke out the finest wine and toasted one another. I cranked up the player-piano, and then we two danced to real music, in the glare of candlelight, for we two had, laughing, lit every candle in the place, placing some of them in the hands, or even, mockingly, in puddles of melted wax, on the heads of the numerous dead who lined the walls and filled most of the booths and chairs of V——'s establishment.

And when V—— came downstairs, wide-eyed, in his night-gown, to discover what all the racket was, we only laughed again and called on him to join the party. We seized him by either hand, and dragged him around and around, calling on him to dance like there was no tomorrow, and he danced, or lurched and shambled, to describe it more accurately, at least until he managed to break away and scramble upstairs again, wailing in terror.

What more? Yes, there was more.

We rang doorbells. We summoned the respectable citizens into the streets at a most improper hour, and we called on them to liberate themselves, to dance, to sing, to make noises, to behave shockingly.

For a time it seemed they would. The revolution seemed to have taken hold. Out with the old, the stagnant, the ridiculously cheerless, in with the cheerfully ridiculous!

Children in particular were willing...to do whatever was to be done, whatever they could imagine. One small boy even *knocked the hat off* a corpse posed in a window!

And—still *more.* We two ascended the clock-tower and caused the bell to ring *at the wrong time.* Unscheduled, violated, the wooden figures rose from their coffins and went through their gyrations on the little balcony before the clock-face, while the two of us, with awesome acrobatic skill, joined them in their dance, switching their removable, wooden hats around and even wearing them ourselves, making a mockery of it all.

Then, with some degree of solemnity, before the assembled multitude, from atop the clock-tower, in a strident, inspiring oration, my amazing companion called on the people to rid themselves of their *most precious possession,* which is their fear. She pleaded with them to have the courage to smash it, like an ugly glass thing.

At last, we two retired to my quarters behind the Town Hall, and *naked,* I climbed into bed with her, and we made passionate love. Afterwards, she told me of a strange country I can almost recall, where the sun rises in the morning, unshrouded, where the sky is often blue, where the living are alive and the dead in the ground, and there are lands to live in beyond the boundaries of a little, fog-shrouded seaport town.

She explained that if I tried very hard, if I cast off my own fear and *dreamed* it, I could *awaken* into that world.

"Do it," she said. "For me."

"I have never felt alive before now," I replied.

"Nor have I," she said.

And so we slept in one another's arms until late in the morning, and we dreamed that we had indeed awakened into the other, brighter world.

So it is concluded, and sealed away in the Secret Archives of the Town, never to be gazed upon by any person, save those of exceptional moral fortitude, with the express permission of the unseen government.

III

But then the clock-bell thunders, and the whole room shakes with it. I hear the mutter of voices and the tread of many feet on the stairway outside.

Instantly I sit up, and comprehend my doom. A *full understanding* of my folly comes to me in a flash.

To think that the dull clods in our town were *capable* of sharing what I have discovered—*that* is madness! To *presume* that the others possess the sufficiently *exquisite sensibility* to appreciate love, or the courage to cast away fear—for *that* I deserve everything that is to befall me. Thus existence cleanses itself!

In an instant, the door crashes open and the redoubtable V— enters, accompanied by many others. He snatches up and dons the pewter-buttoned coat and the bicorn hat (which used to be my father's), and *he* gesticulates wildly with my cane, wordlessly directing the townspeople to drag me naked out of bed, to haul me down the stairs and through the chill, damp streets in the early morning fog, to hold me fast before the tribunal of substantial citizens (including the redoubtable

V——, the punctual Mr. K——, J—— the taximan, Mrs. Z——, and the schoolteacher), where I am to be condemned *without words*, because my crimes are truly and literally *unspeakable*.

I turn once, to look after my lover, but she is only lying in the bed where I left her, naked, limp, her skin as exquisite as near-translucent marble.

IV

hat more can I say? I did not dream it.

I could not understand, save to appreciate that I, too, had failed to cast aside my most precious possession, for I was very much afraid, in the fog-bound morning of a day, which, by the subtle pause in the rhythm of life, everyone in our town knew had arrived.

Naked, I lay on the docks, bound hand and foot, humiliated in every possible manner, my head shaven and covered with grey mud, ridiculous designs traced all over my body, to await the arrival of the dead, and those who deliver them, who would know what to do with me.

EPISODE TWO

THEY ARE STILL DANCING

I awaken, slowly, out of a deeply troubled sleep to the sound of the redoubtable V—— rattling and rapping at my door. The room drifts into dull focus: the grey light of dawn through the soiled windowpane, the mildewed curtains, the bicorn hat of my office on the wooden table, my predecessor's overlarge coat draped over a chair, and the silhouette of V—— at the door, alternately tapping with his knuckles on the glass or rattling the doorknob.

"Please, Sir!" he mutters, then, raising his voice, nearly shouts. "Please, Sir! Come at once."

All around me, the corpses, with whom I share the tiny apartment, seem to nod in silent agreement. Yes, I am needed. Time to get up. My dreams, such as I can remember them, were bright and filled with fire. The waking world, as always, is damp, dark, crowded. The nameless dead line my walls, forty-seven of them at last count, evenly divided between twenty-three men, twenty-three women, and one infant, which, for lack of any other place, I keep in a breadbox in the windowsill.

"Please, Sir!"

Grunting with the exertion, I force myself to my feet and make my way carefully to the door, stepping gingerly over the outflung or stiffened limbs of my various "guests." I wrap myself in an old robe, and, for some semblance of propriety, don my official hat.

I unlock the door, and there is V——, standing in the uncertain dawn. Behind him, the fog veils but does not quite conceal the green dome of the Town Hall and white tower of the Mayor's residence.

"Yes? What is it?"

"It has happened again, Sir. *Perversion.*"

I nod perfunctorily and close the door in his face, not even considering the matter of courtesy or lack thereof because of the simple logic that there are just too many dead people crowded into my apartment for me to have room for living visitors. Besides, I represent the authority of the unseen government and don't have to explain myself. It is only by certain acrobatics, difficult at my age and weight, that I change into my official uniform and my predecessor's ill-fitting black coat with its impressive array of tarnished buttons. I don't know how he managed, occupying these same quarters. He was, I am told, a taller man than myself, and somewhat younger. He thought too much. He got into trouble. I know better. I am grateful to him only for his cane, which he left behind. He used it as a swagger stick. Sometimes, when my joints trouble me, I use it as a third leg.

Thus prepared, I am ready to face the world.

Outside, V——, the tavern-keeper, an illustrious citizen of our town, is waiting patiently, as he knows he has to.

It is only as we make our way carefully down the exterior stairs, stepping over the corpses that have increasingly congregated there, that V—— ventures to speak again. "I can't explain. You'll have to see for yourself. It's *horrible!*"

"Indeed," I reply noncommittally.

I know that some things are indeed horrible and many more, reputed to be, actually are not. The sin of my predecessor, his own *perversion,* about which no one will speak, which has brought a veil of amnesia as impenetrable as any of our never-quite-lifting fogs over the minds of hundreds of witnesses (perhaps myself among them)—now *that m*ust have been horrible.

At the bottom of the stairs, I nervously tap my stick against the handrail.

I am told, or have dreamed, or have heard it whispered, that my predecessor fell in love with a corpse, and *danced* with it before hundreds of witnesses, proclaiming all sorts of ridiculous notions before he was duly disposed of.

Above me, the Town-Hall clock strikes the hour of six, and the familiar, life-sized wooden figures creak through their perambulations before the clock face—the reaper, the sower, the man with the shovel, the coachman driving his hearse—even as, daily, with increasing pain and shortness of breath, I creak through mine.

But V—— has little patience with the infirmities of age and seems, paradoxically, all the more *impatient* in his obsequiousness as he urges me on.

I follow. Shadows are still deep in the narrow, steep streets that lead down toward the harbor. We wind through alleys. At times I have lost track of where we are, but V—— leads me on. The only person up at this hour is the tireless G——_, who wheels the corpse of an old, naked woman about in his wheelbarrow. He has strewn the corpse with purple flowers, for decency's sake. I've heard that sometimes he tries to sell the flowers, with little success. I cannot let that concern me now.

At last we reach V——'s shuttered establishment. He makes a great display of unlocking the door himself, though he knows that I, as a minister of the unseen government, carry a universal key which will open any door in our town.

Inside, in the darkened common room, where numerous corpses slump on the benches or over the tables, and more crowd the shelves, he whispers, "It happened *in the night.* Of course I couldn't have seen anything. Curfew, you know."

There is no need to reply. Of course I know. It is my official duty to know. The unseen government has decreed what are called *internal curfews,* which means that the likes of V—— are confined to their bedrooms.

We descend into V——'s cellar, and he unlocks another door. He strikes a match and lights a lantern, then holds the lantern aloft, swinging it this way and that, doing his pathetic best to illuminate the whole matter, as if the evidence were plain to see.

Forty or fifty pale-faced, glassy-eyed corpses fill the room, piled like cordwood, heaped atop a couple barrels, leaning against the wall on an old bench, with another row seated in the laps of the first.

"Well—?"

"They have *moved.* In the night. When I and my wife were upstairs. They *moved.*"

"How can you be so sure?"

"I have *dreamed* it, Sir."

"Ah." I am restrained from ridicule by the fading memories of my own dreams, which I cannot describe, but which I know, too, were disturbing. Yet now I am awake. I am a rational person, on whose rationality our town and the unseen government depend for the essential *changelessness* which is the bulwark of our lives. I pride myself on this. Unlike my predecessor, who turned out to be some kind of evil lunatic, I am a good man, a firm one, a rational one, who will do his duty, maintain order, and provide comfort to the citizenry as they perform their immemorial duty to the undecaying dead.

Therefore I snatch the lantern out of my companion's hand. I play the detective. I examine the muddy streaks on the stone floor, the position of the corpses, the way their clothing is folded or hangs or has mildewed, and as I do my confidence begins to erode. It is like that frightening, dimly-remembered dream from which I am still not certain I have fully awakened. *Here* is the corpse of an old woman whose buttocks and side are soaked with black mud. The black mud comes from where a rivulet of water has leaked in through the tiny, iron-barred window that opens into a window-well. There is a similar puddle on the floor below the window. But this woman is *on the other side of the room*, as if she got up, staggered to join the company opposite her, and politely bade them move aside to make room for her. This *cannot be*.

I turn sharply to the startled V—— as if to demand an explanation, and all he can say is, "I dreamed that they were *dancing*." Then he puts his hand to his mouth, like a child trying to catch an utterance that has already escaped.

And I am outraged, but quietly. I maintain my sense of decorum. I merely glare at him, as if it is his fault that I begin to remember some of my own dream.

It is only much later, nearly ten o'clock, as I walk along the wharves, that I am calm again. I have spent the last few hours behaving nervously, barking orders to people. I commanded a woman to sweep her doorstep, when she was already doing so. I told the shoemaker, in his shop, to work on the right shoe first, not the left. He obeyed. I waved my cane and sent the singing pedicab driver (who, to his credit, never missed a note) laboring with his load of corpses up a steep alley to my left. I don't know where he was originally going. I don't care. It will work itself out, as those of us who serve the unseen government know things eventually do.

Now my mind is clear again. Here, on these wooden docks, where our lives have such meaning as they do. Here, where at certain irregular intervals one *feels* coming on the way one feels the onset of rain, ships appear out of the fog and, in the night, the dead are offloaded in great heaps like fish. As these ancient planks creak beneath my feet, as I accept the salutes of the scurrying citizenry, I am able to bring my mind into sufficient focus to weigh the problem carefully.

All seems to have proceeded from a dream, but this does not invalidate the truth, for even in dreams does the unseen government supervise every detail of our existence. Dreaming, then, I awoke one morning still weighed down with dread from the fading memory of whatever I might have witnessed while asleep. In this befuddled state, my prior life forgotten, I discovered myself in the loft at the top of the stairs, behind the clock tower adjoining the Town Hall. I saw my predecessor's bicorn hat, coat, and cane left out for me, and understood what office I had now assumed. It was likewise my understanding that I was not the *direct* successor, that the redoubtable V—— had actually held the position for a short time during the emergency, as the *pervert* was disposed of, but it was ultimately the will of the unseen government that I should fill the post, and V—— should return to his tavern-keeping.

Therefore I and not V—— will have to deal with the present crisis.

Clearly, corpses do not move themselves, and it is unthinkable that, once the citizens have carried them from the docks and placed them in their homes or shops or workplaces, anyone should move them. Yet throughout the day I look into troubled faces. No one is so bold as V——, to address me directly. Perhaps they are afraid of being accused, of being dealt with like the *pervert* who formerly defamed my office and nearly shattered the spiritual well-being of the entire community (until partial amnesia set in, like a merciful fog); but I can see it in their eyes. The confectioner gazes out at me from the bay window of his shop (where several corpses sit, apparently enjoying his wares), then turns away furtively as I pass. Pedestrians on the street likewise glance into my face, longingly, then quickly look somewhere else. A few mutter abrupt words, "Nice day, Sir." "All is well, I see." "Getting a bit crowded, Sir, but we'll manage," and similar pleasantries and pieties.

I spend some of the afternoon in the town library, which is a musty, dark room in the basement of the Town Hall, which few ever frequent. There I page through musty, damp-stained volumes which hint at worlds other than our own—filled with brightly-colored pictures of green fields, blues skies, and fiery apparitions like those in my dreams—in search of clues, or philosophical comfort, or anything relevant. This will not do. I am an old man with profound responsibilities, dawdling his time away, and I know it.

Once more I adjourn to the streets, determined to set things right. I peer in through the window of our town's single-room schoolhouse, where the children and the teacher must stand during lessons, because all the chairs are occupied by the dead. I observe that the entranceway is so crowded with corpses that the children must have to squirm through them to get inside. How the teacher does it I cannot imagine.

I smash the schoolroom window with my cane, brushing away the shards, leaving only a bare wooden frame.

All faces turn toward me, expectant, silent.

"Go in and out through the window from now on," I say.

I wonder. Have the dead here also moved? Why has this secret been kept from me? Who dares to conspire? *Perverts?* I will have an answer. There will be an investigation.

Back in my loft, after supper in V——'s tavern, I engage in my own secret *foible*. It is a mild thing, never a *perversion*. I don't fall in love with the dead, nor do I dance with them, but I do talk to them sometimes. I hope the unseen government will forgive an old man's foolishness, but at times I feel very much alone—I have never married, or else I am a widower; I can't recall which—and it is necessary to make my own accumulation of mute guests my audience for long monologues, which I would not dignify by the name of *philosophical discourses*—remembering that my predecessor was quite the intellectual, and look where that got *him*. Nevertheless, to focus my mind, to work out problems in the performance of my duties, I must speak. I begin with the courtesies. I greet my silent guests. I ask them how their day has been. There are the complaints. *Madame, can you keep your child quiet?* Not that I have any way of knowing if any of the women present ever had anything to do with the baby in the breadbox. But I do not *touch* them any more than one does, inadvertently, fumbling about in the dark, or losing one's balance (as one does increasingly with age).

This evening, I sit down, exhausted, in the sole unoccupied chair, place cane and bicorn hat on the table, and address my assembled multitudes, "Well? What do you think? What comes next?"

Outside, the Town Hall clock strikes curfew, the wooden figures creaking through their rounds. From where I sit I can hear the mechanism working.

"Well?" I say again.

My room-mates offer few suggestions. They haven't thought about the situation very much. It would be, in some circumstances, comic. But none of us is laughing.

There's a corpse in my bed that I don't remember being there before, a bloated, fat woman with a gaping mouth and a face like the belly of an enormous fish that has started to go bad. Indeed, she occupies the bed entirely, leaving no room for me. Did I *ever* sleep there myself? Perhaps not. I can't remember.

I doze at the table, with my head down, one hand on my cane.

And in the night, in the dream from which I am not sure I have ever awakened, I hear the music.

A voice whispers, "*Please Sir, come at once. It's happened again.*"

I jerk awake in my chair. The room is dark, silent.

Then I hear it. Laughter, soft, secretive, but laughter. And from somewhere far away, *music,* horns, a drum, tambourines, a muted clanging and banging more like a march than a dance.

I am stunned. I sit there in utter stupefaction. I endeavor to arouse righteous wrath within myself, but, in truth, I am merely afraid. This is not proper. It is not orderly.

I stand up, cane in hand, official hat on my head.

And I hear the laughter again, *from within the loft…*

I jerk awake in my chair, and, trembling, as if to shake off the dream from which I am never certain I have awakened, the dream which is existence itself, I gesture menacingly with my cane at the silent company around me. I don my official hat. I rise to my not totally unimpressive height (the hat and the fact that I represent the unseen government both make me seem taller) and, although it is against regulations *even for me* during the present regime of *indoor curfews,* I step outside onto the landing and observe a rare enough phenomenon, that a full moon has nearly bored through the perpetual overcast and the *green dome* of the Town Hall and beyond it the *white tower* of the Mayor's residence gleam as if lit from within by spectral light; but on the stairs below and through the streets of the town I also observe something completely impossible.

The dead are moving. Gracefully, like wisps of cloud, they glide down the stairs, into the street, though they are not ghosts; no they are solid enough; yet I, who am alive, seem gross and clumsy by comparison.

Struggling for a sense of outrage, cane tapping furiously, I make my way down. Even the wooden clock-tower figures, now motionless in their wooden coffins by the stairs, below the clock face, open their painted eyes as I pass. Impossible.

But in the streets, the dead are dancing. The best I can do is impersonate one of them. The mud-stained woman from V——'s tavern takes me by the hand and leads me through the streets, into the great square before the Town Hall. I can't really hear the music. It is almost like a fading memory even as I experience it, faint jangles of drum, tambourine, and horn, but the others, I am certain, can *hear* it *clearly,* as they move around the square in a great, stately pavane. It is only when the wooden figures in the clock-tower arouse themselves, and strike the hour of midnight even though it is not midnight, but much later, that a change comes over the assembled company, as if an intelligence ripples through them like a soft tide, and I alone, the clod, the idiot, the laggard, cannot sense it. But the muddy, dead woman takes pity on me and once more leads me into the procession the others have formed.

I the detective, the official of the unseen government, the rational man, must pretend to go along with this to uncover the great secret—

Yes, the secret, and why will *you say that I am mad, or that I was dreaming?* (Outraged, I jerk awake in my chair in the loft, don hat, snatch up cane, and come hobbling down the stairs, across the square, down the steep, narrow streets toward the harbor to behold the appalling spectacle.)

In the interests of duty, then, I have violated the *indoor curfew* and joined with the dead, and discovered their innermost secret, which is that on certain nights, such as this one, it is *they* who are alive, while the respectable residents of our town sleep or cower in their beds. It is they who move by some rhythm I cannot share, the mass of them as inevitable as an outgoing tide, pouring from all the houses and alleys and establishments of our town, scrambling out through the window I recently broke in the schoolhouse, until they are assembled on the wharves for some inexpressible communion…and *it is not midnight, but almost dawn* when the ships appear, like black islands far away across the water, and the motor launches set out from them, bearing the great multitudes of the newly arrived dead, *whom we have come to meet,* whose secrets we will now share…but I alone *cannot,* like a single blind and deaf and dumb soul in a mass of the beatific elect. I weep. I wail. I gnash my teeth. No one pays any attention to me, not even the muddy woman from V——'s basement room.

I know what is going on here! It is *forbidden.* The unseen government surely would not allow them to *remember* the sunrise, the world of brilliant blue skies, the sea-birds, white and brilliant, soaring over our heads in the morning light, shouting with incredible voices.

No, it would be horrible *beyond words* if that were true, if the dead were able to experience what the living could not, even for a sequence of hours like a stately pavane on a certain night and morning.

It is *forbidden* and it *cannot be* and therefore it *is not,* as the fog rolls in once more (and there is no moon visible overhead) and the darkness resumes, and the newly arrived dead are left in heaps like fish on the docks (where, in the morning, the citizens will gather them up and take them into their homes); and there is no music at all; and the dancers fade away into thin air to resume their rightful places in attics and cellars and shop windows and schoolrooms.

That which is impossible, which is forbidden, which cannot be, and therefore is not, lingers only in the memory of a dream as I awaken with a start in my chair in the loft, surrounded by the dead. I see that the redoubtable V—— has entered through the unlocked door, seething with rage. He takes up the bicorn hat from off the tabletop and places it ceremoniously on his own head.

Now he glares down me, from the great height of his authority, as he doubtless did at my predecessor, and whispers the single word, *"Pervert,"* as if that is the terminal thunderclap of my existence.

But I have other ideas. He has no right to accuse *me,* merely because he has discovered me with the muddy woman from his cellar seated at my feet, with her head leaning against my lap while, fondly, I run my fingers through her hair and listen to her whispering of things I have certainly forgotten and which she and I, in some other time and place, might even have shared: blue skies, laughter, music—

How could V—— understand any of this? Frankly I find him insufferable, a prig.

He thinks he will dismiss me. *I* think he has usurped this office once before in a similar "emergency" and he's getting *entirely too fond of it.* Therefore I rise. I take in hand the cane I inherited from my predecessor. V—— is willing to grant the infirmities of my age this much, and is therefore caught unawares when, with a single *whack!* I smash his temple with the cane and knock him and the bicorn hat to the floor.

I have to stoop. It is a slow, painful effort, but I retrieve the hat, then, with it in hand, bow sweepingly to my guests, thank them for the pleasant evening we have shared, and explain that I must be off about my duties.

Outside, a few citizens stir in the streets. The wooden clocktower figures rise creaking from their coffins, circling up their mechanical track, to strike the hour.

And I too must make an ascent. I get out a spyglass from the pocket of my voluminous coat. It is a secret of my office, something only officials of the unseen government know, that the government of our town is *not entirely unseen,* but, if you stand on the landing outside the door and point the official spyglass which I found in my predecessor's pocket at the very pinnacle of the *white tower* which is the Mayor's residence, you can discern, through a tiny window, the *Mayor himself,* or at least the silken top-hat he wears as the sign of *his* office. He sits with his back to the window, in a high-backed chair, so you only see the hat, and if you watch for a long time, sometimes you can see it turn or nod. That is all. That is quite enough. I have foreknowledge that the ascent is difficult, especially for one of my age and girth, that in places there are no stairs, and one climbs grasping iron rungs while dangling over terrifying heights. I know that there are *no corpses* in the *white tower,* that it is a conduit to another world, which the dead have remembered to me so beautifully and so passionately. I know that the Mayor waits there, as guardian and gatekeeper and judge, that he waits for us all, and I, now, must ascend and explain myself to him.

EPISODE THREE

THE ORDER OF THINGS MUST BE PRESERVED

It was the dampness that she hated more than anything else, the musty smell of crumbling plaster, of peeling wallpaper, of the very air itself inside the schoolroom, which seemed to cling to her disagreeably.

The numerous corpses, which occupied all the students' seats and even her own, which sat along the walls of the room as if giving her more rapt attention than her living charges—the very dead which lay stacked in such profusion in the corridor outside that one actually had to *touch* them when making one's way into the schoolroom—*those* were damp too. They almost seemed to sweat at times, even as their clothing (if they still had clothing) mildewed and rotted away.

The dead themselves would never rot away, of course, being part of the immemorial *order of things,* that Miss R——, the teacher, had devoted her life to preserving. *The inevitable, inert flesh of the dead is eternal,* was one of the lessons she pounded into her charges. When the children wriggled (as they had until recently, until a *reform* was made) into the schoolroom and sat or stood among the dead, it was Miss R——'s duty to reinforce such precepts. It wasn't that she liked children. No, she despised them, as she despised the clinging damp. She could resist the damp by bathing as little as possible, by using dry powders which gave her person a musty, dry smell of its own. Against the children, her only defense was her heavy stick, which she *thwacked* onto her desktop again and again, while leading recitals of such important phrases as *The order of things must be preserved!*

She regarded herself, despite everything, as a kind and generous person, a selfless person who devoted herself to this important duty above all else. After all, she could point out, there were many, many dents in the surface of her desk, and few on the heads of her charges.

There were none at all on the flesh of the dead, of course, for it was they who were to be preserved above all else, by the will of the unseen government.

Therefore the children sat or stood or crouched, glum and wide-eyed, while she directed them through their lessons, while the dead, everywhere, seemed to laugh silently, or nod in agreement, or mock, or just ignore her.

The air was very close.

Then came the sudden change, the *reform—Crash! Smash!* She turned, amazed and found herself face-to-face with the man in the bicorn hat, the old, fat, slightly lame gentleman, who walked the streets of the town and *represented the authority of the unseen government.* He had shattered the schoolroom window with his cane.

The children turned too, but did not react, waiting for direction from her. She could only gape, and make little wordless sounds.

"There!" the man said. "Use the window from now on!"

And away he went. She leaned out the window and gazed after him with admiration and longing, but she could not bring herself to cry out. Instead, she merely accepted what had happened. She explained to her charges that henceforth they should enter the schoolroom through the broken window, which could not be closed or repaired regardless of the weather, since it was the directive of the unseen government that it remain open.

Primly, she picked out the remaining bits of glass from the window frame, lest anyone cut themselves, which would be disorderly. It was only then that she noticed that her own hand was cut. She clutched her musty dress to make the bleeding stop.

This *reform* had been instituted, she later appreciated, precisely when it was needed, for it was only two or three evenings later that there came into her mind the unspoken certainty which all citizens of the town shared, something halfway between a vividly remembered dream and an incomprehensible compulsion. She knew that each and every one of them would rise at dawn and file wordlessly down through the steep, narrow streets to the great wharves, where, in the night, great quantities of the newly-delivered dead had been left in heaps like fish in a market. It was her duty, and everyone's duty, as the man in the bicorn hat oversaw, to select one or more corpses for herself, and to take them back to her quarters (for she lived in a little loft above the schoolroom) and find a place for them.

That morning, as the fog thinned away, as the distant ships from which the dead had been unloaded faded from view as if they had been part of the fog, a particular zeal came over her.

She loaded a dead child into her hand-wagon, then another, then an old woman, and wheeled them back to her place, dragging each of them into the hallway outside the schoolroom and leaving them with so many of their fellows. Then she returned to the docks for another load, and another, while the man in the bicorn hat smiled at her benignly (and she was *thrilled* at his attention, though she dared not acknowledge it so boldly as with an actual word or gesture). She labored all day, and when she was done, she felt the pride that a mason feels when he slides the very last stone into place. The old entranceway to the schoolroom was completely packed, solid with corpses, so that no more than a serpent could have squeezed through.

With great foresight, then, the man in the bicorn had broken the window. Such was the benevolence of the unseen government to those who preserved the order of things.

That night, she lay, exhausted, on her back on the schoolroom desk, clutching her stick (which she thought of as her scepter) amid the crowd of the dead, in perfect darkness. She thought back over the events of the day, the events of several days, well aware that she, with her extraordinary sense of *order* and the need to preserve it, could sense the passage and pattern of time in the way that few others could.

She was, arguably, the only person in town who did more than drift through the fog of existence. Hers was no eternal, featureless present. She was perhaps the only one (other than the unseen government itself, no doubt) who could think in the past tense.

But that night, she felt an unease, a sense of timelessness, as in a dream she drifted through a clear blue sky, formless, without her stick in hand, with no voice to cry out.

She awoke with a grunt, feeling damp, startled to discover that the children had already assumed their positions throughout the classroom.

They must have crawled in at dawn, as soon as curfew ended. They must have seen her asleep on the desk, but had enough sense not to disturb her.

Patiently, they waited, while the sun shone dimly through the fog outside, the room lightened to a dull grey, and the faces of the almost countless dead were again discernable.

But all was not as it should be. One child, a boy, was out of his place. He stood trembling before the desk. He did not dare look up into her face (as well he should not). She saw that, like an increasing number of children in the class, he was emaciated, barefoot, and filthy. She supposed that poverty was part of the order of things, which was to be preserved by the design of the unseen government, and did not question the boy's appearance, but what *did not* fit into this scenario was that the boy dared stand before her holding a shiny, silk *top hat,* which he had no business ever putting his grubby, rat-like paws on.

She sat up on the desk, slid her legs around, and stood.

"How dare—?"

"Please…" The boy blubbered. Tears and a runny nose left streaks on his dirty face. "I…I found it. In the street. It *fell from the sky.* The others saw it too."

He looked around for support from his classmates, but no other child would meet his gaze.

She snatched the top hat out of his hands.

"I thought I should give it to you right away," the boy said softly.

She realized that she did not know the child's name. She seldom bothered to learn the children's names. But she felt a certain satisfaction that this one had, apparently, absorbed his lessons well.

She poked him away from herself with her stick. Sobbing, shuffling, the boy took up his proper place against the wall, between the slumping corpses of two old women whose faces were drawn in perpetual grins.

"The order of things!" she shouted, pounding on the desktop with her stick with more emphasis than usual, *"must be preserved!"*

The children shouted in reply. She and her charges recited the lesson back and forth, until it gained a half sing-song quality, yet rumbling, like thunder as a storm rises.

All the day she held the top hat in her free hand, sometimes tapping it against the desk top or against her thigh.

None of the children acknowledged it in any way, for it was a new thing, and she had not taught them any lesson about it, and new things, they knew, did not preserve the order.

Yet she herself could not preserve the order either, and once the children were gone for the day (crawling, one by one, out the broken window), she sat for a long time on her desk, holding the hat by the brim, turning it in her hands, considering the implications of the child's claim that it had *fallen from the sky.* That was, she knew, like an image out of a dream, and dreams, unless they were sent explicitly by the unseen government, were not part of the order of things. Therefore she always tried to forget her own dreams, appreciating, educated person that she was, the paradox that it was hard to forget something you concentrated on forgetting.

Any less energetic approach to life would not preserve the order. She had trained herself to forget things by sheer force of will.

Nevertheless, the hat, a solid, real object, was here in her hands. She trembled and sighed at the implications of it. The hat disturbed her so much that, to her own amazement, *even though it was after curfew*, she crawled out of the broken window herself and dropped into the street.

Now her heart was racing. She, herself, was in violation of the order, a *pervert*, as such people were called. She knew there had been a lot of *perversion* of late. Why, the predecessor of the man in the bicorn hat, a former functionary of the unseen government himself, had, somehow, in ways that could not be described or quite imagined, *defiled* his office, so that he had to be replaced by the present, more trustworthy official.

Perhaps she had once known, or even witnessed the predecessor's horrible acts, but through sheer force of will managed to forget them.

Now, in a kind of daze, she made her way through the cobblestoned streets, keeping to the shadows, repeating to herself over and over that what she did was for the best, to *preserve* the order, not to destroy it, that the present emergency—for *emergency* it surely was, that such a thing could happen—justified her actions.

More than anything else she thought of the man she had so admired from afar, the man in the bicorn hat, who personified in her mind the very order itself. *He* would know what all this meant. *He* would know what to do.

He would sit with her, patiently, and explain everything in a calm, quiet way. Perhaps, to comfort her, he would even take her hand in his, as…as…as a father might take his daughter's hand to comfort her. She liked to believe that the man was old enough to be her father, for all she feared that, on the rare occasions she peered into a mirror, the mirror would betray her.

She knew where he lived. What she had to do, then, was reach his dwelling before anything else happened, before she fell asleep and started to *dream* with the knowledge of what she held in her hands.

For if top hats fell out of the sky for grubby children to find, then what was to become of the *order of things?*

The person of her desires, the man in the bicorn hat, resided, she knew, in an official residence of sorts, a loft behind the Town Hall, near the *green dome* beyond which one could glimpse the *white tower* wherein the unseen government itself was purported to gather.

Now, in the darkness, she dared to approach the base of the stairs, which wound behind the clock tower adjoining the Town Hall. Her man lived up there. She'd climb up, knock on his door, beg his forbearance, and explain what had happened.

He would understand, she knew.

She put her hand on the railing and mounted the first step. Something moved above her, but it was only a pigeon, on the ledge before the clock face.

She began to climb, stepping over a corpse.

She heard wooden gears creaking. She gazed up in horror and saw, before the clock face, moving wooden figures. She knew them, of course. Everyone in the town knew that at the *appointed times,* these automatons would rise from their coffins set in the side of the tower, make a gear-driven circuit, and perform their circumambulations before the clock-face itself. They were as familiar as her own hands or face, stiff, trembling, with their once-bright paint faded and peeling: the reaper, the sower, the hearse-driver with his whip upraised.

They came before the clock face every day at the appointed times, *but this was not the appointed time.*

Yet the clock struck, and what followed could only have been a dream.

She heard impossible *laughter* from the loft at the top of the stairs, as if there were much *merrymaking,* which could only represent a *perversion* of the way things should be, quite impossible if her man, the supreme object of her desires, *were still there.*

But what if he were not?

Now her courage failed. She retreated, back down the stairs. Somehow it seemed that the *animate dead* were all around her, like graceful wisps of smoke, yet solid at the same time. It was a paradox her mind could not resolve, because the unseen government, in all its wisdom, had never issued instructions on the matter.

The dead spun her around, as if to drag her into a whirlpool of a dance. She clung desperately to the top hat, afraid she'd lose it, that a corpse would snatch it from her as she had snatched it from that filthy child.

Such things did not happen in the *order of things*, she knew. Therefore she was dreaming. Therefore she was mad. Therefore she was a *pervert*, who had violated the order by her mere presence.

She looked up the stairs again, yearning for her man to descend, despite the hour, with the symbols of his office, his bicorn hat, his heavy coat with the tarnished buttons, and his cane. He would know what to do. He would preserve the order. Perhaps he would even be angry with her, rightfully so, for breaking curfew, *pervert* that she had become. Perhaps in righteous wrath he would beat her with his cane, pounding the order of things into her once more as she pounded it into her charges (but mostly into her desktop) with her own stick. (Where was her stick anyway? She felt helpless without it.)

Even though he might (justifiably) look on her with loathing, her heart went out to him. She pitied him, for the ceaseless burden of his duties, yet looked to him for guidance even yet. She saw him as a naked giant, holding up the whole world. (*That* image must have come from a book.) She loved him very much. Yet she dared not confront him, not now, not this night of all nights. She would have to explain. She couldn't. That would make her *irredeemable* in his eyes, and she could not bear that.

Around her, the dead laughed, and danced.

At last she was able to break away and crawl under the stairs. She groped in the darkness, encountering several corpses. They were disagreeably cold and damp, their clothing like old, rotten paper which tore away when she brushed against them, but at least they *did not move* as she found a space for herself and huddled among them.

With no other recourse, she *put the top hat on her own head*, and remained there throughout the night, alternately dreaming and, *within the dream*, forcing herself to forget that same dream by sheer fervor of will.

What was she to do? A top hat had fallen out of the sky. It was for her to deal with it, somehow, that the order might be preserved.

She awoke, *or dreamed that she awoke*, in the grey fog of dawn. Trembling, weeping softly, with the top hat still on her head, she once more climbed the stairs. She passed the painted clock-tower figures, now asleep in their coffins, soon to be roused at the *proper hour* to summon the citizens from their houses.

Silently she climbed, stepping over corpses. Silently she stood before the door at the top of the stairs, struggling to summon the courage to knock, thinking back over all the times she had watched and admired the man in the bicorn hat through her schoolroom window.

Quickly, she snatched the blasphemous top hat off her own head and held it in her hands, in both hands, as the child had done, twirling the brim around and around nervously.

Then she noticed that the door was already ajar.

She pressed against it with her elbow and dared to enter the room.

She called out, but there was no answer. In terror she stood there, certain that she would be branded a *pervert* for merely being there, but as the day slowly lightened, she saw that there was *no one in the room* but for numerous corpses,

most noticeably an enormous, nude fat woman who occupied the entirety of the bed, a mud-stained old woman in a
filthy nightgown, curled as if asleep on the floor in front of
an empty chair by a bare table, and, shockingly, an eminent
citizen of the town, the redoubtable tavern-keeper V——, lying beneath the windowsill, the whole side of his face covered with dark blood. He had been dead for, she somehow
knew, several days at least. His flesh, unlike that of the other
corpses, had begun to bloat. She grasped for meaning, as she
stood over him, holding the top hat. He couldn't have seen it
fall. He had been *murdered* before then. She tried to fit these
two facts together, as if to arrive at some final solution, but
they were like pieces of a wooden puzzle that, *perversely,*
didn't fit even though every other piece was already in place.

She concludes that this is the work of perverts, and that
it is for her, despite her fallen state, her own moral lapses, to
restore the order of things.

The fat woman on the bed seems to be laughing at her.

No, that cannot be. She is mad. She is dreaming. Corpses
do not laugh. Not out loud anyway.

The dead woman's hand seems to be pointing.

There. On a little stand by the open door. A spyglass. It
is an *official instrument*, which she has seen her man use before, and his predecessor before him.

She stands on the landing, hat on her head once more,
spyglass in her hand. She peers into the distance, at the very
summit of the white tower, now privy to the little-known fact
that under precisely the right circumstances, with precisely
the correct equipment (i.e., this official spyglass), the unseen
government *is not entirely unseen.*

There, at the top. A tiny window. The Lord Mayor's residence. Someone sees her. Someone is waving. She knows
what she has to do.

Hastily, then, she makes her way past the *green dome*, to the base of the *white tower*. She finds her way inside, and begins a perilous ascent. There are no corpses inside the tower, only dust and loose stones which sometimes fall at her touch, crashing and echoing, and an occasional raven which caws from the rafters. Up and around, up and around she climbs a spiral staircase for hours. Sometimes there is no staircase at all, and she must cling to no more than iron rungs, dangling from a dizzy and terrifying height.

But at last she reaches the top. A trapdoor *opens for her,* and the man of her dreams, the man in the bicorn hat, in the official coat with the many buttons, whose example has always been an inspiration to her, is waiting there for her. Beyond words, weeping, she falls to her knees, clinging to his legs.

Then, gently, he takes the silk top hat off her head, sets it on a desktop by his side, and takes *both her hands in his,* and raises her up, until they are *face to face.* She is trembling. She must close her eyes. But she can't. His gaze, she decides, is both stern and kindly, as should be the personification of the unseen government.

"Your loyalty is commendable," he says soothingly. "You have done precisely the right thing in coming to me."

He releases her. She steps back, gasping.

"Yes, yes," is all she can reply. "I thought…the order…"

"…must be preserved. No one knows about this, no one except the two of us?"

"A child found it… He has no idea what it means…"

"Nor can he ever. Nor can anyone," the man says, directing her to the other end of the long, brightly lit room. She gasps in amazement at the brilliant blue sky outside the window. They are above the clouds, above the perpetual fog she has known all her life. A cool, clean breeze ripples curtains.

"Look here," he continues. By the far window is a high-backed chair with its back toward her, as if someone positioned it there to gaze into the heavens beyond. Now the man takes the top hat and places it on *something,* so that, for an instant it seems as if someone is indeed sitting in that chair, hidden from view but for the top of the top hat, which nods slightly.

"The order must be preserved," her man says, and piously she replies, "Yes, it must."

"That the order may be preserved," he says, "it is necessary that the people of the town *look up* to persons in my position, even as I, or my predecessor or successor, might use the *official spyglass* to gaze up to this very window and be reassured by a fleeting glimpse of the *visible embodiment* of the unseen government, the Lord Mayor himself, wearing his top hat, at work at his desk."

She is almost speechless, like a frightened child in her own class. "The—the—"

"Oh yes," he says, laughing. "*The Lord Mayor himself*! Allow me to introduce you."

She can only let out a little cry as he suddenly turns the chair around to reveal hat atop a mop handle, the mop set in a bucket. The hat totters in the breeze.

To her utter amazement, he then removes his own bicorn hat, tosses it contemptuously aside, lifts the top hat from off the mop handle, tosses mop and bucket, clattering, to the floor, *and places the Lord Mayor's top hat on his own head.*

At the very end, she comes to three conclusions in quick succession. The first is that he does not love her, that he never did, that the gleam in his eye and the spirit animating his speech and his manner are closely related to the froth at the edges of his mouth. He is completely mad.

The second conclusion is that the room has been unoccupied for some time, as evidenced by the papers blown all over the floor, the books fallen from the shelves, and even the (inhabited) bird's nest atop one of the filing cabinets.

The third conclusion is that the order must be preserved. She mouths this truism aloud one last time.

The mayor apparently agrees with her. "No one must *ever* know," he says, as he turns suddenly and shoves her out the open window to her death before taking his place in the high-backed chair.

EPISODE FOUR

THE BOY WHO DREAMED
OF NOTHING AT ALL

Because the order of things must always be preserved, the boy accepted the fact that he had no name, even as he accepted that he was always hungry and cold; that he had no shoes, his clothes were rags; and he only got to wash, very infrequently, in rain-barrels. These things were as they had always been. Day after day throughout all the life he could remember, he had squatted or stood with his fellows, in the crowded schoolroom among the numerous corpses, which filled the chairs and lay slumped over the desks, lined the walls in untidy heaps, and so crammed the corridor out-side that the way had become completely impassible. Lately everyone had entered the school through a broken window, ever since the man in the bicorn hat, who represented the unseen government, had suddenly smashed the window with his cane during the middle of a lesson and commanded them to do so.

This "reform" had come just in time, as their teacher, the fierce, malodorous Mrs. R——, never tired of telling them, as she would pound on her desktop (and occasionally on a luckless student) with her stick and lead them in the recitation of such things as, "The order of things must be preserved!" and "All things are as they always have been and as they must be!" which constituted the entirety of their lessons.

But for once, he realized, the unseen government had made a *change* in the changeless order which was to be preserved, because now they entered through the window, as they had *not done before,* and the entrance to the schoolroom *had become* so solidly packed with the silent, grinning dead that nothing larger than a serpent could have come in that way.

It was a paradox he had spent considerable time and effort trying to work out, without success.

Like his teacher, the boy had the almost unique ability among the inhabitants of the town (so she had remarked about herself, in one of her occasional, rambling discourses, never deigning to acknowledge his existence) to think in the past tense. He could *remember*, rather than merely drift through life in an eternal present.

He wasn't sure what it was good for. Mostly he could remember the town dark with an overcast that never quite cleared, the stones of the pavement and of walls dark, and the sloping rooftops dripping with moisture that the sun would never drive away. He remembered, always, the countless, undecaying multitudes of the dead, which the townspeople, by some mysterious compulsion of the unseen government which came to them in dreams, would periodically gather from the wharves and wheel or drag away, to find room for them in their houses, their shops, or in such places as the schoolroom.

The only progression he could remember in his life was that there were always more corpses than before; that, for instance, the two fat, nearly naked men with handlebar moustaches who leaned against either side of the teacher's desk like bookends had not always been there. Getting them through the window must have constituted, for Mrs. R——, a masterpiece of effort and planning. How exactly she had done it, the boy had no idea, but he was certain she had, and he knew that he ought to admire her for it.

She preserved the order of things, above all else, because there *was* nothing else. Therefore, her actions must be, by definition, good.

But somehow he never felt the requisite enthusiasm, because he was hungry, and tired, and alone, because he had nowhere to go when the school day ended and the parents of the other children came for them.

He was afraid that he himself did not fit into the order of things. He wished that he actually could drift through existence in an *eternal present tense,* as Mrs. R—— contemptuously described the other people of the town doing, without any memory at all.

But he remembered how he would rise from where he slept among the corpses in the schoolroom, crawl out the window, and wander through the dark and empty streets of the town, in the very last hour of the night, still during curfew (which never seemed to apply to him; that, too, was part of the order of things). He would peer into shop windows, where corpses were arranged wearing the finest, warm clothing, or seated around tables, enjoying cakes. He knew that he could never have such cakes himself, but sometimes he stole soggy bread from bird-feeders. Once in a very great while, he found that someone had left a glass of milk out on a ledge. He eagerly drank it down, without knowing why it was there or who it was actually intended for.

He was afraid, because of that. His conscience troubled him. Was he part of the order of things, or was he like the piece left over when the puzzle is perfectly assembled? What happened to such a superfluous piece? He imagined Mrs. R——'s great, heavy stick crashing down on the tabletop, like a hammer crushing a nutshell.

Once in a very, very great while, the offering on the windowsill was wine, which he also drank, though he was certain it was not intended for him, and it made him sick and light-headed.

But the wine made him see things. Perhaps that was its purpose, and his.

He stood one morning, in the cold, light rain, little more than a spray but enough to soak him through and plaster his unkempt hair to his forehead. He'd had nothing to eat for several days, but now a sip from the windowsill made his throat burn and his head spin. He clung to a lamp-post, just to remain upright. For a while the icy stones and the damp air made his feet and his bare legs (for there was not much left of his trousers) burn with cold, but then a warmth seemed to settle through him and he was able to let go of the lamp-post and make his way to the center of a market square, and stand still, more or less steadily. By some compulsion, he leaned his head back, and looked up. Rain fell on his face, at first cold, then soft and warm and caressing; and then there was no rain at all, only a brightness that dazzled his eyes, as if the long-fabled sun (which he'd heard about in stories) were actually going to come out.

He saw, for an instant, a perfect, white, brilliant nothingness.

But then there was a blemish in it, a speck of black, which grew and swirled and toppled as it did, assuming some kind of rapidly-tumbling shape his eyes could not quite make out.

Then the black thing hit him in the face, not hard, but sufficient to knock him over backwards into a puddle; and he lay there, drifting, as if on a raft in the dark, oily harbor, as the brightness overhead receded and the sky became slate-grey, as it always had been. (And so the order of things was preserved.)

He was aware, as he lay on his back in the puddle, that he held the black thing in his hands, that it was light in weight, and made of stiff cloth, and smooth to the touch.

He heard someone singing, bellowing really, completely off-key. A wheel clattered right past his ear. Mud splattered into his face. The caterwauling voice was familiar, of course. He knew that J——, the taximan, pedaled corpses throughout the town in his pedicab, singing as he went, often pointing out the sights to them as if they were tourists. J—— had doubtless perceived him lying there as one more corpse, whose function was perhaps to fill a hole in the pavement. He could easily have run over him.

But that wasn't right. It subtly defied the order of things. The boy considered the object he now grasped, which likewise could have been crushed under a stray wheel: a silken *top hat,* finer than anything he had ever held in his hands, albeit now smeared with mud.

It was not right. Wearily, the boy rolled over onto his side, then lurched up onto his knees, kneeling in filthy water. He examined the hat more closely, marveling at the sheer incongruity of such a thing being touched by his dirty fingers.

He almost thought to put the hat on his own head, though it was much too large for him, and he would have disappeared into it. But he fancied that he heard a wind rushing out of or into (or merely within) the hat. It moaned softly, like wind across the mouth of a broken pipe; but he had no time to wonder at it, for the town was coming awake all around him. Shutters clacked open, and a whole row of old-lady corpses gazed down at him disapprovingly from a high window. A storekeeper opened his shop, and set the corpse of a child— it looked like a girl about his own age, her long black hair knotted with golden bells—rocking gently back and forth in a swing over the door, her bare feet hanging down limply. The shopkeeper paused, and looked at the boy suspiciously. Overhead, the bells jangled.

Some of his own classmates passed by on the way to school, talking softly among themselves, but suddenly shocked and silent when they saw him and what he held in his hands.

Then a deep-voiced bell began to toll, and high above him, high above the square and the shops and the muddy pavement, with a creaking and groaning of machinery, familiar wooden figures lurched out onto the platform before the face of the Town Hall clock. They too were part of the order of things. Every schoolboy knew them: the reaper, the sower, the man with the shovel, the coachman driving his hearse. They had been figured in Mrs. R——'s discourses, as outward manifestations of the forever-praised, unseen government.

What they told him now was that he did not belong where he was. He got to his feet and ran, gasping for breath as he did, clinging to posts and windowsills sometimes so that he would not faint; but with the utmost effort he made his way through back alleys and over fences to the schoolroom, and climbed in the window before any of the other students arrived.

Mrs. R——, the teacher, was already there, astonishingly, incongruously asleep on her desk, stretched out on her back, her great stick clutched in both hands, her eyes squeezed shut as if in anger.

All he could do was stand shamefacedly before her, the hat in his hands, gazing down at his mud-caked toes, trying to formulate some explanation in his mind of how this wonderful top hat, this beautiful thing, was not part of *his* world, how it did not belong, but had *accidentally*—if such a thing were possible, if the unseen government could have allowed it—fallen from heaven, and he had inadvertently polluted it by merely touching it, however necessary that might have been for him to bring it to Mrs. R——'s attention.

One by one, the other children climbed in through the window and took their places, standing or sitting or crouching among the numerous dead. The sky lightened. Even the gloom within the schoolroom retreated.

And Mrs. R—— awoke, and rose before him like a thundering tidal wave of wrath. She sat up, slid her legs around to the front of the desk, and dropped to the floor. Her great stick pounded the floor an inch from the boy's toes. But he did not flinch. He did not look up to meet her gaze.

"How dare—?"

"Please." He began to sob. "I found it. It fell from the *sky—"*

Mrs. R—— snatched the hat out of his hands and poked him in the shoulder with her stick, which sent him sprawling. On hands and knees he made his way over by the wall, and wriggled into his place among the corpses of several old women. Just then the dirt-blackened hand of a gaunt man with a wiry beard, who rested on the shelf above, fell down on the boy's head, as if to comfort him.

The teacher paid him no more heed, and shouted and gesticulated her way through the day's lessons, pounding on the desk top like some fantastic orchestral conductor until finally, because of the vibrations, both of the mustachioed fat men fell over into untidy heaps. All the while she held the top hat in her left hand, her stick in her right, until both seemed to have always been a part of her.

The teacher may have paid the small, nameless, muddy boy no more heed, but the fat kid, B——, took a special notice of him that day. When Mrs. R—— had reached a particular paroxysm of enthusiasm, when her voice shrieked and she foamed at the mouth and reached a level of complete obliviousness to all around her, B—— took the opportunity to crawl over to where the nameless boy sat, crouch down beside him, and whisper into his ear (with foul breath), "I think you're a liar," then flick his finger hard at the back of the boy's ear, again and again, making a *thwacking* sound.

The smaller boy knew that it was no use to ask him to stop, or to bring this to the teacher's attention, as it was part of the order of things, even as it was on those sporadic occasions when food was actually brought into the classroom and lessons paused for lunchtime, and the fat kid would grab two or three portions for himself, punch anyone who objected in the face, and meet no criticism at all from Mrs. R——.

That this was inexplicable was merely part of the order of things, which was, everyone knew, to be preserved.

B—— kept flicking his ear. He was trying, of course, to start a fight, which *would* elicit a response, usually the teacher's stick crashing down on the heads of anyone but the instigator.

Therefore, all the smaller, hungrier boy could do was lean forward into the lap of a corpse and lie very still, while the torment continued. After a while, perhaps, he fainted, or went to sleep and began to dream; and again the vision came to him, a full revelation now, of a clear, blue sky fading into pure featureless white; and this time it was *he* who constituted the one blemish in the pure void, as he fell through it, only he never landed anywhere at all. Instead he seemed to dissipate, like smoke, and the whiteness was utterly clean and empty once again.

When he awoke, the schoolroom was empty of living persons. B—— must have given up torturing him at some point, perhaps even having come to the conclusion that the smaller boy had *died* right then and there; and of course it would have been an unspeakable *perversion* to flick the ears of a corpse and whisper insults to it.

Now he was alone. Now the dead around him left him unmolested, save for the bearded man, whose cold, heavy hand did fall onto the boy's face one more time when he stirred. But it was an easy matter to roll out of a corpse's lap and out of the reach of that dead hand.

He lay on the bare floorboards, shivering and gasping. He felt terribly weak, but his mind was clear, and the room did not shift or sway. He listened to the fading sounds of evening through the broken window, the voices of the last few pedestrians, carriage wheels, and the Town Hall bell ringing as it always did, just before curfew.

There was only silence for a long while afterwards. Gradually he discerned water dripping somewhere inside the schoolroom. But then there was something else, the musical tinkling of many light, tinny bells, a rattle of them, as if a great number of little bells were being dragged through the schoolroom window. There followed a brief moment of eclipse, as something blocked the light from outside.

Then he heard a light footstep, and he looked up and saw the girl he had seen that morning, the one from the swing over the shopkeeper's door. He could only tell, in the dim light, that she was very thin, that the skin of her feet and legs was almost luminescently white, and that she might well have been naked, but for her incredibly long, incredibly luxuriant hair, which covered her whole body down to her knees and which was braided and criss-crossed with strands of thousands of tiny metal bells.

She held out her hand to him, and he took it, staggering to his feet. It wasn't as if she pulled him up. Her touch was firm and warm, but she felt light as a cloud. He couldn't resolve this. He tried not to think.

She said, merely, "Come," and he came with her, out into the silence and the night, where overhead the dim, full moon almost showed its face through the thin overcast. All around him, in the periphery of his vision, shapes moved, flickered, as if the town were, in the darkness, coming awake *again*, not as it did at dawn, but into another order of animation altogether. Trailing shapes, like smoke, like little clouds, separated from the shadows of the alleyways and under the eaves, and began to whisper among themselves, and moan softly like the wind over broken drainpipes.

He and the girl padded silently up the steep, wet streets, she leading him by the hand.

Once, to his astonishment, she paused before a bakery, where corpses sat in the window around a little table, as if enjoying cakes, and she took up a stone from the pavement and smashed the window, then greedily reached in for a handful of cake, which she stuffed into her face.

After a moment's hesitation, he did the same, and the cake tasted better than anything he had ever imagined, but after a moment more, he felt weak again, and ashamed, because he knew this was *not part of the order of things* which was to be preserved; and all he could hope was that he was dreaming, that none of this had ever happened, that he still lay in the schoolroom among the corpses where he belonged and had imagined the whole thing. The alternative was that he had become—*again the changeless order incomprehensibly changed*—what Mrs. R——, in her energetic lectures, labelled a *pervert,* a term she spoke with the utmost loathing.

More than anything else, he wanted to go to Mrs. R——
and explain that he hadn't meant to do anything wrong.

But she wasn't there. The dream, which he knew in his
heart of hearts was nothing of the sort, continued.

There was laughter behind him, and even soft music.
He turned around from the window. The girl with the bells
smiled at him, and the street was filled with *hundreds* of half-
material phantoms, the semi-animate dead, the *impossible,*
the things from dreams, which danced and sang and laughed
as if a great carnival were taking place and all the dark, silent
town now poured out in an expression of faintly-echoing,
mysterious joy.

He thought to run away, but there was nowhere to go.
His legs went wobbly. He noticed that his forearm was cut,
where he'd reached through the smashed window, and he was
bleeding. But that didn't matter. Nothing fit. It wasn't part of
the order of things, which was to be preserved.

Nor was the girl. He was drawn to her. He followed her
willingly, the way he'd grabbed the cake willingly, as a kind
of release from the long misery of his entire life, but at the
same time he was afraid, and fascinated, and amazed, and utterly bewildered, as the great mass of revelers assembled in
the square before the Town Hall to watch the wooden clock-
figures creak through their accustomed courses *at the wrong
time.* Everyone laughed, and made mockery of the Town, of
the order of things, of the clock-figures. Someone, up there
on the platform, was giving a speech of some sort. Someone else danced with the wooden clock-figures, rode on the
hearse waving to the crowd, then snatched off the wooden
coachman's top hat—for an instant the boy was terrified that
the rude fellow would throw the hat down into the crowd,
that it would fall on him; but that didn't happen; the fellow
merely put it on his own head.

The boy followed the girl with the bells. He asked her what her name was, and she said she had no name, any more than he did, any more than anyone did, really, because nothing had names, or places. There was *no order of things* she said, nothing at all, only lies and custom and fabrication. Therefore the two of them could break into fine houses and steal food, or parade about in fine, warm clothing, while the respectable citizens were huddled in their locked bedrooms, because of the *new curfew regulations*—which the boy knew, because Mrs. R—— had ranted about it, had become necessary to preserve the eternal and changeless order of things after certain regrettable episodes of *perversion* by citizens supposedly worthy of trust.

The others in the celebrating crowd laughed at him, and with him, and shared a joke and a song and freely-flowing wine, until he danced and whirled around with them, his head spinning. He didn't know what he said or did. At one point it seemed that the girl with the bells sat down beside him on a bench, and an old woman was with them, and she put her warm, heavy arms around the two of them, and caressed them, and explained (in words that echoed inside his head like a voice out of a dream), that since everything was a *lie,* one imposture was as good as another, and one might as well *join the elite of society* by abandoning one's name, all responsibility and position, and by *impersonating a corpse.* There was even a drug you could take, which would enable you to sleep *without breathing* during the day, to make the charade more convincing.

The one shortcoming was that he had to change from his stolen, warm clothing back into his filthy rags at the end of the night, when the clock-figures emerged once more on their proper schedule to announce the coming of the hours of *order* and *reason* when *laws* and the *unseen government* held sway, and things were as they had always been.

So, in the fading darkness, he stood shivering in his ragged clothing while the clock-figures went through their motions and a bell began to toll; and the woman was gone, and the revelers and dancers faded from the streets like mist. Possibly someone pressed a cup of something into his hand and he drank. For a time the girl stood beside him, holding his hand, and then she wasn't there anymore, and he fell down faint, on his back, into a puddle in the middle of the pavement, all the while sobbing softly and trying to protest that he wasn't a *pervert*, or didn't want to be one anyway, that he loved the *order of things which was to be preserved,* that he wanted nothing more than to return to his place in Mrs. R——'s classroom, and even if the fat kid tormented him or Mrs. R—— beat on him with her stick, that was as it should be. He knew that much. He had learned his lessons well. He was a good boy. He would explain all this to the girl with the bells the next time he saw her, then, perhaps, take *her* to meet Mrs. R—— who would make clear to her that the lies were themselves *lies* and themselves part of the larger order of things.

But that isn't how things work out, not at all. Once more, lying there, he dreams of the pure white void, and it is an *authentic* dream, not to be doubted, a genuine *vision,* like a window opening suddenly. For the longest time, there is sheer, beautiful nothingness without warmth or cold, without sound, without hunger or pain; but then, again, a blemish appears, a speck, something of indiscernible shape, tumbling down toward him, down.

Soaking wet, shivering in the foggy dawn, he sits up in protest, at the very moment that a quite large object crashes with an enormous *splat* into the pavement right in front of him, and something warm rushes over him; and it takes him quite a while to figure out that he is covered with blood, very little of it his own, and that the thing on the pavement before him is none other than *the corpse of Mrs. R——*, who, unbeknownst to him, tried to return the top hat he'd found to its rightful owner, had climbed the *white tower* which rises beyond the *green dome* of the Town Hall and represents the very pinnacle of the authority of the *unseen government,* there confronting the *Lord Mayor himself,* who thanked her very much, proved to be quite mad, and hurled her out a window to her death for her pains.

But the boy doesn't know this. He will never know this. He can only weep as he sees his beloved teacher lying there in the ruin of her own face (which is smeared across the pavement, her teeth scattered like spilled corn), with her limbs all broken and twisted in impossible positions.

The order of things must be preserved, he knows, or if not merely preserved (and here he struggled toward an original thought), *restored.* So the best he can do is take a wheelbarrow from in front of a shop (no one stops him, as if he is invisible) and gather Mrs. R—— up as best he can, scooping up her teeth in his unclean hands. Then, struggling, light-headed and weak, he wheels Mrs. R—— through back streets and alleys until he reaches the schoolroom before any of the students arrive.

It is a sheer masterpiece of planning and effort, mostly effort, which enables him to get Mrs. R—— in through the window, and assembled, more or less, on her desk as if she is sleeping there.

He resumes his position among the clump of dead women by the side wall. The bearded man's hand from the shelf falls down in front of his face once more. Gently, he moves the hand aside, so he can watch as the other students enter and take their places.

None of them dares look directly at Mrs. R——. No one says anything. The fat kid, B——, whimpers softly.

And so the day passes, in the lesson of silence, and *the order of things is preserved.* At the end of the day, the other students leave through the window. But the boy remains alone in the dark. He can hear a few sounds from the outside, from the night-time, sleeping city, perhaps even a few bells, but he does not heed them, certain of his duty now, of his place.

The next day, only a few students return, and the day after that, fewer still. Before long, none.

For a time, someone leaves cake and milk and even wine for him on the windowsill, but only for a short time. Then nothing.

The corpse of Mrs. R——, unlike any other corpse the boy has ever seen, begins to decay, darkening, bloating, the flesh falling away with remarkable speed. He has no idea why. He merely knows that *this* corpse was not delivered from mysterious steamships in the middle of the night to be found in a heap on the town wharf, then gathered up by the citizenry and taken into their homes. This one is different, even as he is different. It is the piece of the puzzle left over when the puzzle is completed, the part that doesn't fit; and it is only gradually that he realizes the wonderful, terrible truth, that *even that which does not fit is part of the order of things,* which is eternally preserved. He lies in his place, among the dead, dreaming of the perfect, changeless void, which is not the negation of the order, but its *culmination.*

In time he is able to hold what is left of Mrs. R——'s skull gently in his lap, and speak to it softly, and show her the flawless, white nothingness which he has discovered.

THE OBSERVATORY COMMITTEE

Delirium is always in the present tense. Only the rational have an awareness of the past.

He can't remember who said that. Possibly one of the corpses. As the Senior Member of the Observatory Committee, it is his job to know that sort of thing, to expound on such matters with wisdom and dignity, and inspire not mere, rote allegiance, but genuine admiration from the other members of the Committee—most especially from the Junior Member, whose insolent attitude is less and less concealed these days.

Now all of them, himself, the Junior Member, and the other four, resplendent in their gleaming, scarlet robes and tall, conical caps (which would look like dunce caps on anyone else, but have, in this context, undeniable *gravitas*) are seated around the long table in the bright, spacious committee room, with its wide, open windows and high ceiling. Outside, the sky is gray and overcast.

The room is relatively free of corpses. True, a fat, dead man in the garb of a carnival king slumps in the high, throne-like chair at the head of the table, some of the other chairs are filled with the dead, and thirty or forty other corpses are heaped like old, lumpy sacks along the walls; but, even so, the Senior Member appreciates the benevolent foresight of the unseen government, which has provided the Committee with this *copious* work space, in an annex behind the *green dome,* adjoining the Town Hall.

Appreciation is their specialty, for it is the immemorial function of the Observatory Committee, which is not actually a part of the unseen government but a supporting body, to *observe* and *appreciate* the efficiency of the government's program: the orderly manner in which the innumerable dead are transported at certain (but mysteriously unpredictable) intervals from the town's docks by cheerful, dutiful citizens, who continue to find (increasingly scarce, yet honorable) places for them in their homes, their shops, and even in public buildings like this one.

An image he encountered in a book somewhere, or heard (or even came up with himself) in the course of some Observatory Committee lecture is that the citizenry are like never-tiring wasps, building their endlessly dense and complex nests, not out of regurgitated wood-pulp, but out of the uncorrupted bodies of the dead, to dwell among them forever.

It's supposed to be beautiful. The Observatory Committee is supposed to appreciate this, and public morale is to be maintained by the knowledge that somewhere, behind closed doors in a lofty annex adjoining the Town Hall, someone actually *does* appreciate it.

But now they are met in a time of crisis. The Order of Things has not been preserved. It is not beautiful.

The six members of the Committee are gathered around their end of the table, turned around or sidewise so they might confront an actual official of the unseen government: the man in the bicorn hat (a tall, lean, stoop-shouldered fellow of middle years, the latest in an increasingly erratic succession of such functionaries) who has steered into the room a wobbly, two-wheeled cart containing a child, a filthy, emaciated boy whose clothing is in such a state of decay that he is almost naked but for a scrap of a blanket wadded up in his lap.

For just a moment Senior Member thinks, hopes, that this is just one more corpse, but the boy's skeletal fingers are clawing at the blanket. Then the boy pivots his head on his impossibly thin neck. Tears stream down his face, cutting pale channels down muddy cheeks. His eyes are wide but not gazing at anything in the room, least of all the Senior Member of the Observatory Committee.

"It's so beautiful," the boy says, sobbing. "So close, so far away—"

"What is beautiful?" the Senior Member asks softly. He attempts calculations, merely so that *reason* may grasp at something; but the boy's age eludes him. Indeterminate. Not old enough to have hair on his bare legs. But his development could be stunted. He looks as if he has been starving for a long long time.

The Senior Member can only await the boy's answer, which comes as an almost inaudible whisper. "Nothing at all, Sir. Just white light. Nothing at all."

"What's so beautiful about *that?*" the Junior Member snaps, his dark eyes doing their best to affix everyone, like a basilisk's gaze, his hatchet-face twitching like a bird's.

"It's empty," the boy says. Then he lowers his head and continues clawing at his blanket. It is clear he will say nothing more.

"Well?" the Junior Member says after several minutes of silence, as if to accuse all others of blithering, imbecile incompetence.

The members turn away. The Senior Member gazes upward, into the chandelier. There are dead children among the strings of crystal. He's not sure how many, three, maybe four. A cluster of little arms hangs down, like the tentacles of a jellyfish in perfectly still water. The faces are so unlike that of the dirty boy: fat and pale, almost bloated, like vacuous cherubs. No meaningful comparisons there.

"Well?" the Junior Member demands, as if this is somehow the Senior Member's fault.

"Indeed, Sir," the man in the bicorn hat says, "the question is properly asked. The matter must be dealt with."

So the Senior Member begins to mentally rehearse a speech, full of sweeping, thundering oratory and wild gesticulations, all about how this issue, this *crisis* is like a cancer, eating away at the very vitals of society; how the Order Which Must be Preserved is all but irreparably threatened by the fact that a cast-off child, a waif, an orphan apparently without a name (for none was ever discovered in the records of the corpse-crammed schoolroom where he was found) might have a vision—and he did not doubt that this was a genuine visionary before him, as mysterious and inscrutable as the unseen government itself— of something *new,* something *other,* something *outside* the Order of Things, something which the Observatory Committee could not observe and therefore not appreciate; how, if this could happen, if the common folk even *dreamed* that behind closed doors such unease had settled in—well, *well?* The question was *well* asked. Even as a great, vaulted ceiling crumbles a little bit at a time, at first, with one piece of plaster falling, then another, long before the catastrophic collapse...*even as the foundations of the Order of Things might so perish* and the next time the dark ships arrived out of the fog and the newly-arrived dead were left like heaps of fish on the docks...*what then?* Would the dead have to *stay there?*

Such is the content of his speech, apocalyptic, terrifying, relentless. Of course he never delivers it. Everybody already knows those things. And his speeches are always best appreciated undelivered, even as the Observatory Committee never reports to the unseen government or harangues the general public. It is sufficient that they *could*. The potential will suffice. After all, the way one gets to be Senior Member is by leaving things deftly unsaid.

To the man in the bicorn hat, he merely replies, "I shall consider this matter."

To the other members, even the glaring Junior, he says nothing at all. The meeting is at an end. All rise, but for the corpses.

ir, the problem does indeed require swift resolution," the stoopshouldered man in the bicorn hat said, his voice somehow steadily cadenced, completely even in tone, like the steady rumble of the wheels of the two-wheeled cart as he and the Senior Member wheeled the dirty boy through the twilit streets. It was almost curfew. Shopkeepers hurriedly closed their windows, took in their signs, rearranged the corpses in their windows or on their doorsteps for the night. The redoubtable J——, the pedicab driver, who often sang to his corpse-passengers and pointed out the sights to them as if he were a tour guide, now peddled by hurriedly, his cab empty, his head down against the gathering cold and damp.

"Sir—" said the man in the bicorn hat again, and then he said nothing at all, and there was no sound at all, and it seemed that the two-wheeled cart continued on of its own accord, with no one to hold up the two poles which were designed to be harnessed to either side of a horse, but which the man in the bicorn hat had gripped in his hands.

The sight of this cart moving of its own accord, with the poles extended before it like the groping feelers of some enormous insect, was curious enough, but more curious still, striking, even *terrifying* for its implied contempt of the Order of Things To be Preserved was the way the dirty child turned around, letting the blanket fall away from him (so that he was almost naked, his every rib and bone in sharp relief) and held up *something* for the Senior Member to see.

"It's beautiful," the boy said. "*So* beautiful."

And for an instant the Senior member could see that it was *not* beautiful, but horrible. The boy held up a human skull, a forbidden object and image in this town. (Pictures of such, where they occurred, had been obliterated from all books in the library, from all textbooks used in the schools.) By the command of the unseen government and by immemorial custom, the dead which were delivered onto the wharves and carried into the houses and shops of the town *did not decay*, but remained forever, the changeless "guests" of animate humanity.

"So beautiful," the boy said. "Look."

And the Senior Member could not help but look, for his mind had been touched, some kind of genuine rapport established. After an instant it seemed that the boy did not hold a skull at all, or any solid object, but had defined by the position of his (upraised) hands, a *void,* a perfect, empty gap in the air, and this *nothingness,* this brilliant light, dispelled the gathering gloom of evening, the mist and the damp. The Senior Member was falling into the white light. It swallowed him and all his world, and, yes, it was very beautiful.

lways in the present tense...

"Well?" the Youngest Member demands angrily.

"Sir," says the man in the bicorn hat, "something must be done. The question is well-asked."

The Senior Member jerks his head back, startled to find himself still in the high-ceilinged committee room.

A draught or vibration makes the chandelier overhead rattle. The dead children's hands wave limply.

"I—"

"Well?"

"Sir, something—"

"I shall consider it," the Senior Member says, and the meeting is at an end. All rise.

The Senior Member follows the man in the bicorn hat, out of the room, along a corridor, down a flight of stairs. The other committee members assist in carrying the cart with the boy in it down the stairs, and in clearing away corpses as needed.

By some transition he cannot follow, as if several paragraphs have suddenly been deleted from the story of his life and he has now lurched ahead, he discovers himself and the man in the bicorn hat well along in their journey through the winding, narrow streets of the town, in the damp and the gathering dark. The cart's wheels rumble steadily, like a voice. The man in the bicorn hat pulls the cart along behind him, one pole in either hand. He says nothing.

The Senior Member, in his red, flowing robe and pointed cap, struggles to keep up. He carries a cane, which punctuates his stride with its tap on the wet cobblestones.

J——, the cabman, pedals by silently, his cab empty.

They pass the school-house where the boy was discovered. No one goes inside anymore. The place is packed solid with corpses. Some of them lean out the broken window. In the street outside, makeshift benches have been set up for the students, boards across barrels, but they are deserted at this hour, their damp surfaces gleaming from the light of a nearby lamp. A corpse lies under one of the benches, as if sleeping there.

Their route has been circuitous. It makes no sense. They come to the base of the stairs that wind around the clock-tower adjoining the Town Hall. Wasn't this where they started?

Never mind. Offering no assistance, the Senior Member can only follow as the man in the bicorn hat lifts the skeletal child out of the cart and begins wading through corpses on his way up the stairs. The Senior Member follows, his cane tapping. He grasps the railing with his free hand and climbs, panting, past the coffin-like niches in the wall of the tower where rest the familiar wooden clock-figures (which he has admired all his life for their grace, their steadfastness). Even as he attains their level, the deep, hidden mechanism within the tower grinds to life and the figures stir, wobbly, weather-beaten, lurching as they move, but still *dutiful*—yes, that is the right word; he would have expounded on this theme had he ever delivered his speech. Even as the beloved figures (which he has gazed upon in wonder since he was a child) of the reaper, the sower, the man with the shovel, and the coachman driving his hearse rise upon their appointed path, around the tower, up to the platform before the clock-face to announce the curfew and the eternal progression of the preserved order—*even now* as they move, something is *odd*, wrong, *amiss*, because it seems to him (as if it has come in a vision, like a flash of white light) that the wooden figures are *laughing*, utterly failing to maintain their usual decorum, their *gravitas*, and that among them, among them, *dancing*, swarming over the appointed pathway, filling up the platform before the clockface as if it were a crowded theatrical stage, are countless diaphanous, half-visible figures, some of them covered with strings of tiny, jangling bells. They don't belong. They are illegal. They violate the order. Yet they flow up into the clock-face like clouds driven before a strong wind, while the windows of the town (which should be darkening, as shutters are closed and lanterns extinguished, according to the established order of things) blaze with brilliant white light.

For an instant, he can only grasp the railing, flail with his cane into the air, and weep with the beauty of it all, and he feels helpless, ridiculous, *obsolete,* desiring above all else to rise into the light, to waft away; but his aged body and his lurid, red robe are too gross, to heavy to do so.

Never mind. By a transition he cannot follow, as if there are definite *lacunae* in the tale of his life, he finds himself, in the damp and the gathering dark, at the top of the stairs, on the platform with the man in the bicorn hat, who hefts the child onto one shoulder to free a hand, so he can rustle around in the pocket of his voluminous overcoat for a chain of keys. He fumbles for a time and unlocks the door to his own quarters.

"You keep it locked?" the Senior Member asks.

"Alas, Sir, there have been irregularities of late."

The door swings wide. Once inside, the man in the bicorn hat draws a smoldering straw out of a coal-box on the floor and uses this to light a candle, then another, then a small lamp.

The senior member follows him into the room, ducking now to avoid hitting his conical cap on the ceiling.

All is as it should be, for the private quarters of such a functionary. They have to wade through corpses to make their way to the far end of the room, where an enormous, fat female corpse covers almost the entire bed. The man in the bicorn hat lowers the dirty child onto the bed, into the dead woman's armpit, as if into her embrace.

Then he turns the single unoccupied chair in the room around and offers the seat to his other guest.

"Very good," says the Senior Member, sitting down wearily. "We must continue our deliberations, and I my meditations. It is as I explained to you."

"You explained to me, Sir?"

"Didn't I?"

"Of course you did, Sir. And now I will leave you, as I must complete my rounds for the evening."

"Yes—yes—but first, tell me."

"Tell you what, Sir?"

"Did you see…anything…as we came up here?"

"Should I have, Sir?"

"Thank you."

"You're welcome, Sir. For what?"

"For being someone I can rely on. The Order needs men like you."

"Very good, Sir." The man in the bicorn hat salutes, then exits, to complete his perambulations.

Alone in the room now, having placed his conical hat on the floor and prodded the dirty boy awake with the tip of his cane, the Senior Member begins the interrogation.

"And so, child, you have been, shall we say…naughty?"

Silence. The boy stares into space, wide-eyed, clutching something beneath his crumpled blanket.

"You are not…happy…"

There is no response.

"Possibly you would like a…snack. I could look around. I am sure I can find some cheese or something…"

Silence. The whole room creaks very slightly, as if settling. Shadows and candlelight flicker over the pale face and bare chest of the boy, and over the numerous corpses.

"Look, we could be friends. We could play a game. I could tell you a story. Then you tell me one? Shall I begin?"

The boy's head bobs downward, like the head of a doll with broken strings.

The Senior Member realizes that he is making little headway. He doesn't understand children. He knows that. The excellent, if somewhat malodorous Mrs. R——, the teacher, used to specialize in that. What has become of her? She has disappeared, and even the Observatory Committee has failed to appreciate the reason why.

In fact, it occurs to him with some sense of fury and despair that he hasn't managed to appreciate much of anything of late, that the other members, particularly the obnoxious, ambitious Youngest, have certainly failed to appreciate *him* as he has struggled with the present crisis.

It is time to reassert his authority. It is time to change his tactics. He must be firm, show his stuff, prove he is still on top of things—

Therefore he poked the boy, hard, with his cane, hard enough to bruise, knocking him backwards, out of the dead woman's armpit.

The boy tumbled to the floor, then rose slowly, with a solemn, but unafraid expression on his face. He held his crumpled blanket in his hands. He stood silently while the Senior Member ranted.

"So, we have been having *visions,* have we, something naughty, something nasty, something *unauthorized,* which *you* in your delirium, your delusion fancy come from *some other source,* as if there *is* another source—a *second government,* unseen even by the first, a Lord Mayor above our Lord Mayor, a King over all, *God*—Well, *well?* What do you think? What do you have to say for yourself? This won't be tolerated, you know—"

Now the boy began to weep softly. He gazed into the Senior Member's eyes as if he had actually noticed him for the first time and desired to confide in him.

"I only say that it is beautiful, Sir, and I want to go away, into the white light, into the empty place."

"Then why don't you?"

"Because it is so beautiful that I want to share it with everyone else."

Now the Senior Member sought to affix him, to impale him on the spear of reason, the shaft of logic, the hurling missile of common sense—

"But if everyone goes there, it won't be empty anymore, will it?"

"Yes, it will," said the boy softly.

"Oh really?" With a flick of his cane, like the motion of a swordblade, the Senior Member snatched the blanket out of the boy's hands, revealing what the boy had been clutching all along, the skull of burning light, the shape which was not a shape, the white void itself, which spoke to him in the familiar voice of the missing teacher, the absent Mrs. R——, who explained to him how very beautiful it all was, this nothingness which had a voice.

Presently, someone is speaking right into his ear.

"Sir, the matter *must* be dealt with?" says the man in the bicorn hat.

"Well, *well?"* demands the endlessly obnoxious Youngest Member, who violates decorum further by moving beyond *potential* and actually delivering the harangue within him: "Well, you stupid, senile, incompetent, imbecile, you haven't got a clue, you're unworthy of your position, your post, your trust, and *I'll have it if I have to gut you like a fish and step over your dead body,* you moron, you fatuous, *corpse-brained* abortion—"

The Senior Member jerks his head back, very much surprised to find himself in the high-windowed committee room. (it is dark outside, but there are sounds of revelry from the streets, and flashes of strange lights.)

He is staring up at the dead children in the chandelier who are, he is certain, mocking him, haranguing him, *blaspheming* against the order of the living and the dead, which is to be preserved at all costs.

Therefore he must rise to the occasion. He will *deal* with the problem before it gets out of hand. Painfully, he creaks to his feet, unsteadily, like a wooden figure on an old, faulty mechanism, but what matters is that he *does it.* He swirls his voluminous red robe like a bull-fighter's cape. (An image from a book somewhere.) He slashes the air with his cane as if it is a sword. Astonished, the members of the Committee, even the Youngest, even the man in the bicorn hat (who is not a member of the Committee) scramble to get out of his way.

"I'll show you how to deal with things! Look!" With all his strength he smashes his cane down into the lap of the dirty boy in the cart. The boy screams. The cart flips over. The Senior Member strikes again and again, not so much at the boy, but at his crumpled blanket. Then he pokes at it, stamps on it, dances a little dance on it (with a vigor belying his years), and finally flips the blanket into the air with a deft flourish of the cane and jabbers, "Nothing there! nothing! nothing! it's all a lie. Nowhere to go! no place but here! no time but now! no tense but the *present!"*

Weeping, from both ecstasy and pain, the dirty boy gazed up at the huffing, panting Senior Member with his upraised cane, and whispered softly, "So very beautiful. You will never *appreciate* that, or be able to *observe* it. I am sorry for you, Sir. I truly am."

The cane descends, like a thunderbolt, like the spear of reason (or of the unseen government, or of God if one has been authorized) in all its wrath, certain to split open the boy's own skull, but before it can there is a burst of light, and the boy is holding the infinitely beautiful *nothingness* in his hands, and he leans forward and *vanishes into it,* as if he'd folded himself into the air, into nothing at all.

But the void is still there, sucking everything into it. The chandelier rattles. The fat, dead children tumble down onto the tabletop, then vanish into the light. The air is full of swirling bits of paper, flying bits of furniture, pictures stripped from the walls.

One by one, as he watches, the members of the Observatory Committee, with expressions of utmost joy on their faces, step into the whirlwind and vanish into the light.

The two-wheeled cart flips over a couple times and follows.

The brilliant light pours in from all the high, open windows, as if the whole town, the whole sky above the town, is ablaze with this inexpressibly beautiful mystery.

And *he alone cannot appreciate it*. He alone is ridiculous, obsolete, like a creaking, wooden figure with its paint peeling, too heavy and gross to rise into the light.

He can only strike with his cane, smash and destroy the enemy of the Order which must be preserved.

If it can be.

And the man in the bicorn hat walks into the light, as if he has patiently waited his turn, and now it is his turn. Exit. The end. He is going with the rest.

Not so fast.

With a supreme effort, casting his cane aside, the Senior Member tackles the other, knocking his bicorn hat off into the void, but clinging to him in a desperate, passionate embrace. As the two of them tumble under the table, the Senior Member is able to whisper, "I can't let you go. I need you. You're the one person I have always been able to rely on. *Please* don't leave me. I'm *afraid*—"

"Very good, Sir."

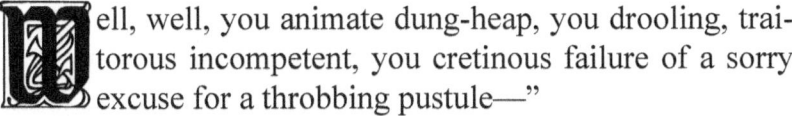ell, well, you animate dung-heap, you drooling, traitorous incompetent, you cretinous failure of a sorry excuse for a throbbing pustule—"

It is the Youngest Member, who hasn't gone anywhere, poking at him *hard* with a broken fragment of his own cane, hard enough to draw blood.

He jerks his head back, and is surprised and dismayed to find himself, not in the high-windowed committee room, but in the cramped quarters of the man in the bicorn hat (who is out on his perambulations, or has been sucked into the brilliant void, or lies half-senseless under a table in the committee room, elsewhere) seated among the corpses. One of the candles and the lamp have gone out. The remaining candle sputters. It too will soon fail.

For an instant—he is not really sure; it might be a trick of the light, or the memory of a dream fading—it seems that the dirty boy is still there, the look on his face one of sadness and compassion. The boy shakes his head gently, then the last candle goes out and there is only darkness.

ell, *well—?*"

The Youngest Member yanks the door open, flooding the corpse-crammed room at the top of the stairs with pale light. Boldly, he wades in, among the corpses, and grabs the Senior Member by the ear as if he were a child. He drags him out onto the landing and demands, one last time, spittle splattering into the Senior Member's ear.

"What *are* you going to do about it?"

"This," says the Senior Member softly, as he snatches the broken piece of his cane out of the Youngest Member's hand and rams it into his gut so hard that it sticks out his back. The Youngest Member makes an astonished, croaking sound, then a high squeal as the Senior Member lifts him up over the railing and sends him tumbling into a pile of corpses below.

"Well," says the Senior Member. "*Well.*"

Perhaps he should feel a sense of satisfaction, about what precisely he is no longer certain. He can make no sense out of the continuity of events anymore, as if more than a few paragraphs were deleted from the tale of his life: instead, whole pages, entire chapters.

In the dawn's light, then, the Senior (and only) Member of the Observatory Committee waited on the landing until his friend, the man in the bicorn hat, joined him.

"The matter must be dealt with," the man said.

"Yes. I understand."

He understood that he would go on in his appointed path, like the creaking wooden figures that (even now) crept their way up the side of the clock-tower, toward the clock-face, to announce the coming of another day and the preservation of order. If only he were like one of them, there would be no puzzlement, no pain, no accounting for the fact that through some inexplicable revelation or vision, the *entire living population* of the town had vanished overnight, but for the two of them.

They came upon J——'s abandoned pedicab in the street, tumbled atop a pile of corpses. It would be useful, they both realized. On the way down to the wharves, the man in the bicorn hat pedaled, and the Senior Member rode as a passenger.

But there was no room for him on the way back, of course, after they had come to the water's edge and seen the line of black freighters fading away into the vanishing fog, and beheld the great heaps of the dead that covered the wharves, like fish piled at the market.

The two of them heaved an old woman (clad only in a burlap sack, her bare, blue-grey feet sticking out) into the back of the pedicab, followed by three children, and a dwarf with an enormous moustache.

It was as good a combination as any, for them to wheel back up into the town, the man in the bicorn hat pedaling, the Senior Member of the Observatory Committee pushing from behind. They had to start somewhere, if the order of things, as decreed once again by the unseen government, was to be preserved.